You Are Special

You Are Special

Neighborly Wisdom
from Mister Rogers

By Fred Rogers

RUNNING PRESS
PHILADELPHIA · LONDON

Library of Congress Cataloging-in-Publication Number 2001118710
ISBN 0-7624-1247-X

This book may be ordered by mail from the publisher.
Please include $1.00 for postage and handling.
But try your bookstore first!

Running Press Book Publishers
125 South Twenty-second Street
Philadelphia, Pennsylvania 19103-4399

Visit us on the web!
www.runningpress.com

Contents

Dear Neighbor,

There never has been, and there never will be in all of creation, another person exactly like you. "You are special." This is a message you've probably heard in many ways through our television "visits" as well as from the caring people in your own real life. "You are special" is not just something we need to hear as children. It's an essential message for "growing" people of all ages . . . and in all neighborhoods.

Each one of us has certain strengths. Each one of us has certain weaknesses. Each one of us is special . . . you and each person you happen to meet.

I've learned so much from many teachers. Of course, some of them didn't think of themselves as "teachers." Nevertheless, I've loved learning all through my life; and, now through this book, I'm really pleased to share some of those things that I have thought about for a long time.

When I was just five years

old, I discovered that I could easily express my feelings through my fingers at the piano. As an adult, I find writing melodies and lyrics for our television programs to be an important way to express a wide range of emotions and ideas. The themes of some of those songs have turned out to be a natural way to organize

the quotations in this book.
You'll find them at the begin-
ning and end of each chapter.

You'll bring your own
personal experiences to every
page of this book, and that's
what will enrich these words
beyond measure. I'm always
fascinated to hear the many
creative ways that people use
what they read and hear.

Once you've read the words
in this book and made them
your own, may they find their
place inside of you—and
nourish that essential part
of you that inspires you to be
the special person you are.

Fred Rogers

You Are
Special

You Are Special · You Are
Special · You · Are Special · You
re Special · You Are Special
u Are Special · You · Are
pecial · You Are Special · You
re Special · You Are Special

You Are Special · You Are
pecial · You Are Special · You
re Special · You Are Special
u Are Special · You · Are
pecial · You Are Special · You
Special · You Are Special

"You Are Special"

♩ . . . You are my friend

You're special to me.

There's only one in this

wonderful world

You are special . . . ♪

There never has been . . .
and there never will
be—in the history of
the earth—another
person exactly like you!

NEIGHBORHOOD TROLLEY

Each one of us is much more than any one thing. A sick child is more than a sickness. A person with a disability is more than a handicap. A pediatrician is more than a medical doctor . . .

You're much more than
your job description or
your age or your income
or your anything else.

Each generation, in its turn, is a link between all that has gone before and all that comes after. Our parents took from their parents and gave us what they were able to give, and we took from them what we could and made it part of ourselves. All that, and much more, helped to make us who we are.

My hunch is that anyone who has ever graduated from a university, anyone who has ever been able to sustain a good work, has had at least one person—and often many—who have believed in him or her. We just don't get to be competent human beings without a lot of different investments from others.

Have you had people
who have touched
you—not moved
you in order to
manipulate you—
but touched you
inside-to-inside?

Take a minute to think of at
least one person who has
helped you become who you
are today . . . someone you
feel has really accepted the
essence of your being. Just
one minute . . . one minute
to think of anyone who has
made a real difference in
your life.

The greatest gift
you ever give is
the gift of your
honest self.

Shyness isn't something that just children feel. Anybody can feel shy. And one reason we feel that way is that we're not sure other people will like us just the way we are.

Early on, I was allowed to play on the piano whatever I was feeling. If, instead, my parents had said, "Oh, don't play that loud, ugly stuff, play something pretty and happy," I might have given up "the musical way" of dealing with my feelings.

There's the good guy and the bad guy in all of us, but knowing that doesn't need to overwhelm us. Whatever we can do to help ourselves—and anybody else—discover that's true can really make a difference in this life.

There's only one
person in the whole
world exactly like
you . . . and people
can like you exactly
as you are.

The real issue in life is not
how many blessings we
have, but what we do with
our blessings. Some people
have many blessings and
hoard them. Some have few
and generously share them.

Redeeming moments can be as brief as the twinkling of an eye—when we human beings can say, "I love you" . . . "I'm proud of you" . . . "I forgive you" . . . "I'm grateful for you." That's what eternity is made of.

We all have
different gifts, so
we all have different
ways of saying to
the world who
we are.

The toughest thing
is to love somebody
who has done
something harmful
to you . . .

especially when
that somebody has
been yourself.

It's what's inside us that matters most.

"It's You I Like"

♪ . . . It's you I like,

The way you are right now,

The way down deep

   inside you,

Not the things that

   hide you . . .

It's you I like . . . ♪

I'm Proud of You · I'm Proud
You · I'm Proud of You · I'm Prou
of You · You
Prou I'm of You
I'm of You
You I'm
of You · I'n
Proud I'oud o
You · I'm Proud of You
Proud of You · I'm Proud o
You · I'm Proud of You · I'm

I'm
Proud of
You

I'm Proud of You · I'm Proud of You · I'm Proud of You · I'm Proud of You · I'm Proud of You · I'm Proud of You · I'm Proud of You · I'm Proud of You · I'm Proud of You · I'm Proud of You · I'm Proud of You · I'm Proud of You · I'm Proud of You · I'm Proud of You · I'm Proud of You · I'm Proud of You · I'm Proud of You · I'm Proud of You · I'm Proud of You ·

"I'm Proud of You"

. . . I'm proud of you.

I hope that you're

    learning how

    important you are,

How important each

    person you see can be.

Discovering each

one's specialty

Is the most important

learning . . . ♪

Whether we're a preschooler
or a young teen, a graduating
college senior or a retired
person, we human beings all
want to know that we're
acceptable, that our being
alive somehow makes a
difference in the lives
of others.

I'm proud of you for
standing for something you
believe in—something that
isn't particularly popular,
but something which assures
the rights of someone
less fortunate than you.

I'm proud of you for
the times you came
in second, or third,
or fourth, but what
you did was the
best you had
ever done.

I'm proud of you for the times you've said "yes" when all it meant was extra work for you and was seemingly helpful only to somebody else.

I'm proud of you for the times you've said "no" when all it seemed to mean was a loss of pleasure, yet eventually supported the growth of somebody else as well as yourself.

There is no normal life
that is free of pain.
I'm proud of you for
times you wrestled
with your problems
and discovered how
much that helped
you to grow.

"You're Growing"

♪ . . . I like the way
    you're growing up
It's fun that's all.
You're growing
You're growing
You're growing in and out.
You're growing
You're growing
You're growing all about . . . ♪

You've Got to Do It

You've Got to Do It · You've
ot to Do It · You've Got to Do
· You've Got to Do It · You've
Got to Do It · You've Got to Do
· You've Got to Do It · You've
ot to Do It · You've Got to Do
You've Got to Do It · You've Got
u It · You've Got to Do It · You've
to Do It · You've Got to Do It
ot to Do It · You've Got to Do It
u It · You've Got to Do It · You've
to Do It · You've Got to Do It

"You've Got to Do It"

. . . It's not easy to keep
   trying, but it's one good
   way to grow.
It's not easy to keep learning,
   but I know that this is so;
When you've tried and learned
   you're bigger than you
   were a day ago.
It's not easy to keep trying,
   but it's one way to grow.

You've got to do it.
Every little bit,
    you've got to do it. . .
And when you're through,
you can know who did it.
For you did it, you did it,
    you did it . . . ♪

We don't always succeed in what we try—certainly not by the world's standards—but I think you'll find it's the willingness to keep trying that matters most.

It's not the honors and the prizes and the fancy outsides of life which ultimately nourish our souls. It's the knowing that we can be trusted, that we never have to fear the truth, that the bedrock of our very being is good stuff.

Asking for help
is not a sign of
weakness. In fact,
it can be a sign
of real strength.

When we're able to
resign ourselves to the
wishes that will never
come true, there can be
enormous energies
available within us for
whatever we *can* do.

The thing I remember best about "successful people" I've met is their obvious delight in what they do. And their delight seems to have very little to do with the trappings of worldly success.

One of the most
important things
a person can learn
to do is to make
something out of
whatever he or she
happens to have
at the moment.

There are all kinds of artists in the world. If people can combine the talent that they have inside of them with the hard work that it takes to develop it, they can become a true artist of some kind.

In order to be an
inventor, we have to
be able to imagine
something before
we can make it.

Play can be one of
the most valuable
tools for creative
problem-solving . . .
all our lives.

Some of my richest experiences have come out of the most painful times . . . those that were the hardest to believe would ever turn into anything positive.

Someone scrawled the following
on the bulletin board of that
great Notre Dame Cathedral:
"Le monde demain appartiendra
a ceux qui lui ont apporté
la plus grande espérance."
(The world tomorrow will
belong to those who brought
it the greatest hope.)

Transitions can be times of growth, but they can bring feelings of loss. To get somewhere new, we may have to leave somewhere else behind.

You rarely have time for everything you want in this life, so you need to make choices. Hopefully your choices can come from a deep sense of who you are and who you want to become.

It's true that we take a great deal of our own upbringing into our adult lives; but it's true, too, that we can change some of those things that we would like to change. It can be hard, but it can be done.

"Please Don't Think It's Funny"

♪ . . . In the long, long trip of growing
There are stops along the way
For thoughts of all the
    soft things
And a look at yesterday.
For a chance to fill our feelings
With comfort and with ease
And then tell the new tomorrow,
"You can come now when
    you please."

So please don't think it's funny
When you want an extra kiss.
There are lots and lots of people
Who sometimes feel like this.
Please don't think it's funny
When you want the ones
    you miss.
There are lots and lots of people
Who sometimes feel like this . . . ♪

There Are
Many Ways
to Say
I Love You

There Are Many Ways to Say I Love You · There Are Many Ways to Say I Love You · There Are Many Ways to Say I Love You · There Are Many Ways to Say I Love You · There Are Many

There Are Many Ways to Say I Love You · There Are Many Ways to Say I Love You · There Are Many Ways to Say I Love You · There Are Many Ways

"Many Ways"

. . . You'll find many
   ways to say I love you.
You'll find many ways to
understand what love is.
Many ways, many ways,
Many ways to say
   I love you.

Singing, Cleaning,

Drawing, Being

Understanding,

Love you . . . ♪

One of the most
essential ways
of saying, "I love
you," is by being a
compassionate
listener.

You don't ever have to do anything sensational in order to love or to be loved. The real drama of life (that which matters most) is rarely center stage.

Taking good care of others when they need it is one way to show your love. Another way is letting others take good care of you when you need it.

When we love a person we
accept all of that person:
the strong with the fearful,
the true mixed in with
the façade. And the only
way we can do that is by
accepting ourselves
that way.

You bring all you
ever were and are
to any relationship
you have today.

It's frightening to feel that sadness may never go away. Sometimes it's hard to remember that "The very same people who are sad sometimes are the very same people who are glad sometimes."

I remember, after my grandfather's death, seeing Dad in the hall with tears streaming down his face. I don't think I had ever seen my father cry before. I'm glad I did see him, though. It helped me know that it was okay for men to cry. Many years later, when Dad himself died, I cried; and way down deep I knew he would have said it was all right.

Solitude is different
from loneliness.
Solitude doesn't
have to be a lonely
kind of thing.

Certainly, the desire to be like the people they love shapes children's earliest values.

Caring comes from the Gothic word *kara,* which means "to lament." So caring is not what a powerful person gives to a weaker one. Caring is a matter of being there . . . lamenting right along with the one who hurts.

"I Think of You"

♪ . . . When the day turns
into night
And you're way beyond
my sight,
I think of you,
I think of you.

When the night turns
into day

And you still are far away
I think of you,
    I think of you.

Even when you are not here
We still can be so
    very near.
I want you to know,
    my dear,
I think of you . . . ♪

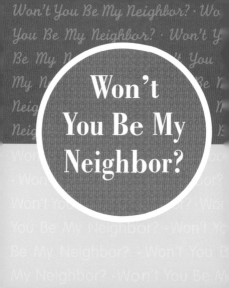

Won't You Be My Neighbor? · Won't You
My Neighbor? · Won't You Be My
ighbor? · Won't You Be My Neighbor?
Von't You Be My Neighbor? · Won't
u Be My Neighbor? · Won't You Be My
ighbor? · Won't You Be My Neighbor?
on't You Be My Neighbor? · Won't You
My Neighbor? · Won't You Be My
eighbor? · Won't You Be My Neighbor?
Von't You Be My Neighbor? · Won't You
 My Neighbor? · Won't You Be My
eighbor? · Won't You Be My Neighbor?

"Won't You Be My Neighbor?"

♪ . . . I've always wanted to have
   a neighbor just like you.

I've always wanted to live in
   a neighborhood with you.

Would you be mine?

Could you be mine?

Won't you be my neighbor? . . . ♪

You are special . . .
and so is everyone
else in this world.

You are unique . . .

and so is everyone

else in this world.

There is something
of yourself that
you leave at every
meeting with
another person.

Deep down we know that
what matters in life is much
more than winning for
ourselves. What really
matters is helping others
win, too, even if it means
slowing down and changing
our course now and then.

When the gusty winds
blow and shake our lives,
if we know that people
care about us, we might
bend with the wind . . .
but we won't break.

There is a close relationship between truth and trust.

Anger makes us
feel isolated.

One of my wise teachers, Dr. Orr, told me, "There is only one thing evil cannot stand, and that is forgiveness."

Human beings are so much alike . . . and yet all so different. How comforting to see the endless variety of people: comforting because one person's differences from another show us that it's all right for us to be different in many ways, too.

We all have angry
and even violent
feelings within us, but
most of us learn, as we
grow, how to express those
feelings in ways that
don't hurt ourselves
or anyone else.

When I was a child and
would see scary things
on the news, my mother
would say to me,
"Look for the helpers.
You will always find
people who are helping."

The words for
"thank you" are
probably the
greatest words in
any language.

You make
each day a
special day
by just your
being you.

The older I get, the more
convinced I am that the
space between people
who are trying their best
to understand each other
is hallowed ground.

Love and trust in the space between what's said and what's heard in our life can make all the difference in this world.

"It's Such a Good Feeling"

♪ . . . And when you
   wake up ready to say,
"I think I'll make a
   snappy new day."
It's such a good feeling
A very good feeling,
The feeling you know
   that we're friends . . . ♪

This book has been bound using
handcraft methods and Smyth-sewn
to ensure durability.

The dust jacket and interior were designed by
Alicia Freile.
The text was edited by Melissa Wagner.
The text was set in Abadi, Adobe Garamond,
Clarendon, Bodoni, Briem Script, Cedar Street,
VAG Rounded, Monoline Script, Sonata,
and TF Roux Borders.

Photo Credits:
Jim Judkis: p. 59
Richard Kelly: pp. 3, 17, 24–25,26, 35,
45, 50–51, 62, 66–67, 69, 71, 75, 90–91,
94, 106, 118–119, endpapers
Walt Seng: pp. 15, 87, 103, 110–111, 118–119,
front and back covers
William D. Wade: p. 47